OUR VICTORIAN STALL
FUND RAISING FOR CHARITY

Beverley Birch

Photographs by Nick Birch

Hamish Hamilton London

Imagine a vast glass building standing here. There was one, once. It was called the Crystal Palace. The old photograph shows what it looked like. Now there are only grand steps, broken columns and statues. Just over 50 years ago a fire burned it down. No one really knows how it happened. It's still a mystery.

This place is very near our school. In fact our school is called Paxton Primary after Joseph Paxton, who built Crystal Palace about 140 years ago, in the time of Queen Victoria. At school we're learning about Joseph Paxton and life in Victorian times.

We're trying to work out where we are on the picture. Everyone's got a different idea.

Just as we're exploring the sphinx, the rain pours down. Everything is dark and crumbling, but you can still see how fine it must have been, with statues and long promenades. There were gardens and fountains . . . and grand ladies in sweeping skirts.

Maybe if we just ignore the rain, it will go away and let the sun shine through. There's still a lot of discussion about the picture. 'I'm sure the gardens were down there,' insists David, who's been having a long, hard look at the plan. 'Just look at all the broken urns. They were meant for flowers!'

The next day something else makes us think a lot more about Victorian times. A lady tells us the story of Mary Ellen, who lived over 100 years ago in America. When she was a child the people who looked after her were very cruel to her.

It isn't a pleasant story to hear. But it has a happy ending. Someone found out what was happening, and helped her. He set up a society to rescue other children who were cruelly treated or neglected. Not long after a similar society began in this country.

It is called the NSPCC – the National Society for the Prevention of Cruelty to Children. It began by helping Victorian children. Now, over 100 years later, it still has work to do, protecting children from being ill-treated.

When the lady asks us to help collect money for the NSPCC, we say yes. She gives us a game to play. We have to fill in all the place names on the map and ask people to give us a little money for each one we get right.

In the afternoon, we talk about Crystal Palace again. What skills Joseph Paxton had! He designed and built such an elegant airy place, and not from bricks and stone, but from glass and metal. It was the largest iron-framed building that had ever been made. We do a mime about building it.

David takes his part as Joseph Paxton very seriously.
'You're dropping the glass!' he says.
'Well, don't just stand there, help!' answers Luke. 'Anyway, this is a mime, you're not meant to talk!'

Meanwhile Lewis digs deep holes for the foundations, and Kelly and Alexia carve the statue.

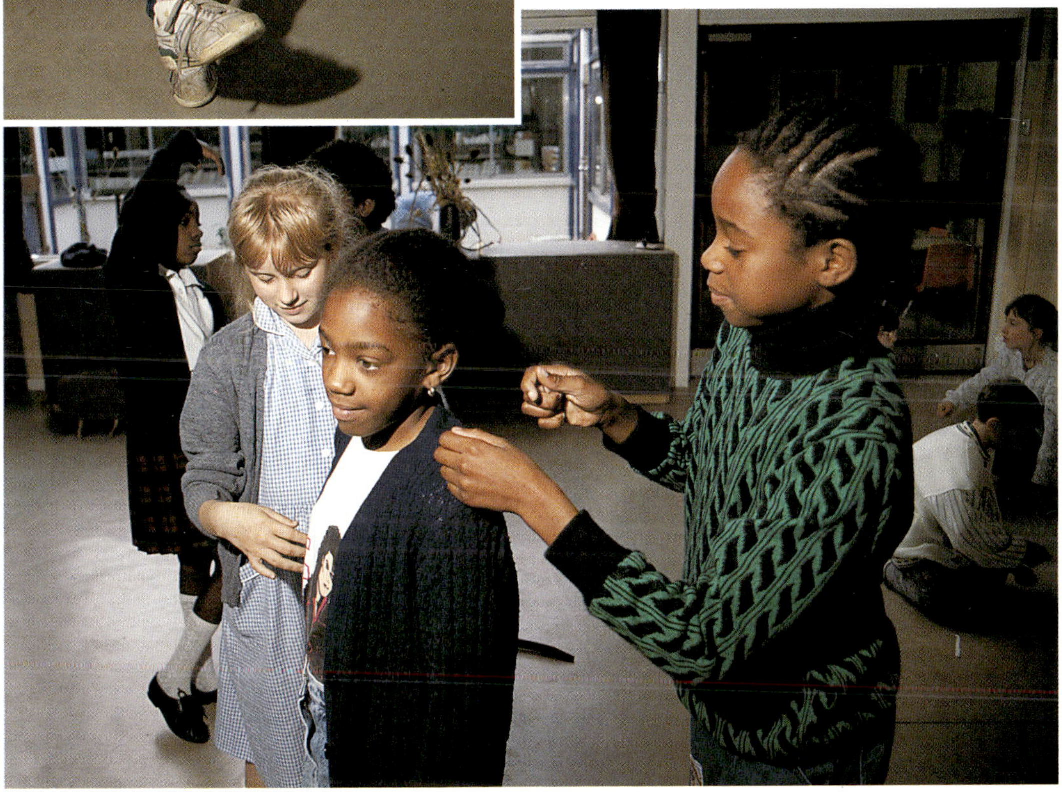

'Look at it burning down!' exclaims DeeJay.

The others have found pictures of poor Victorian children. Sally has found one of a chimney sweep, black with soot from being up the chimney.

'I'm going to write about him being cut and bruised and having his feet pinched to make him go up!' she says.

'And remember that bit we read about working *and* sleeping in the same dirty clothes every day of his life!' adds Kizzy.

'Come and look at this one,' DeeJay shows Sally. 'Imagine going on and on, shovelling for hours and hours . . . never seeing the sun except on Sundays because it's dark when you start work and dark when you stop work!'

Sally is remembering the other things she read, about children forced to crawl under machines to clean the floor, and getting their hair caught in the machinery. And children sent down the mines to pull carts . . .

We've had a week to play the NSPCC game. People have been giving us money for each of the place names we have filled in.
'We've got to hand the leaflets in today,' Dean reminds Sally.
'I couldn't guess this one,' she complains.
'I couldn't either,' says Zoë. 'Or this one.'

We work out how much money we've collected. But we still want to do a bit more. We've found out so much about the lives of Victorian children. *Now* we keep thinking about cruel things happening to children today.

It doesn't take us long to make up our minds. Our school is named after Joseph Paxton, who was a Victorian. And we've been finding out about Victorians all week. We'll do something 'Victorian' now.

We'll make Victorian trinkets and sweets and sell them on a Victorian Stall to raise money for the NSPCC.

The next thing is to plan what we want to make, and how, and when.

There's quite a lot more talking about that!

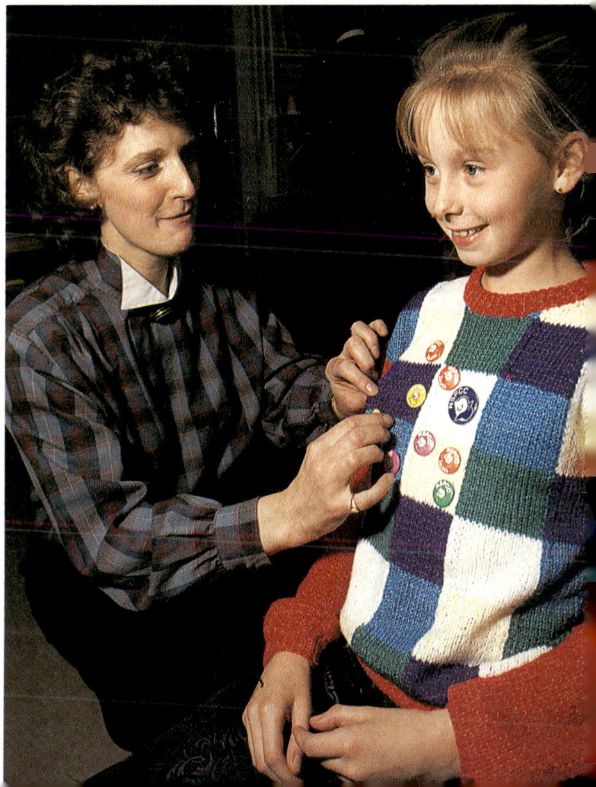

First we make some pincushions. We've collected small plastic pots and bottle tops, scraps of material and cottonwool.

Steven is working fast. He has already stuffed a pot with cottonwool and covered it with material. He has only to decorate it with lace, and it will be finished.

Alexia is trying to decide if she'll add some green braid to hers.

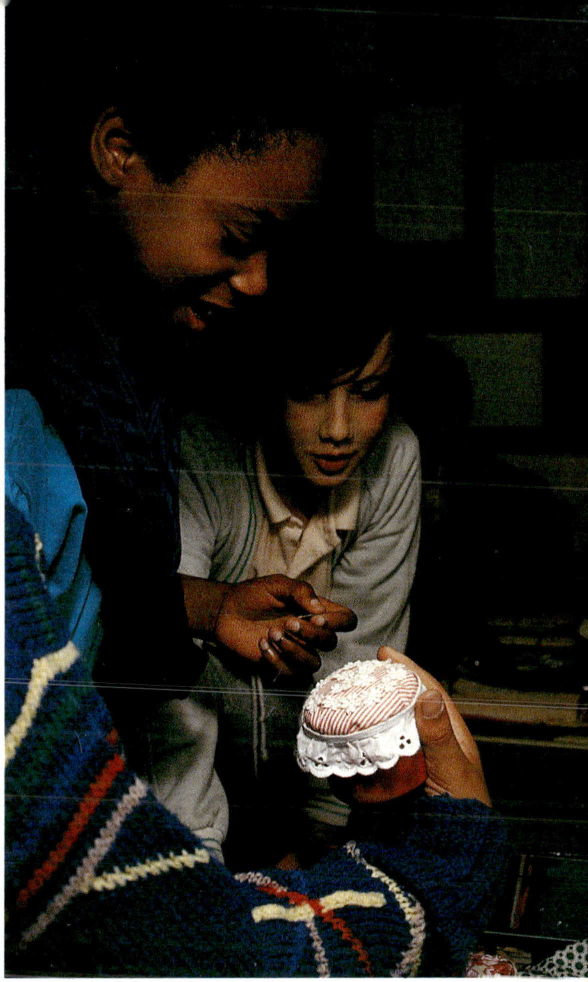

Meanwhile David and Luke's poster is coming along well.

We must have a Victoria sandwich cake as the centrepiece for our Victorian stall. First, we need a shopping trip to buy flour, eggs, sugar, butter, and some jam to put between the layers. David chooses some. 'I like strawberry jam best,' he says.

'This is hard work! I'm tired,' he complains later, stirring the mixture. DeeJay steadies the bowl quickly. The whole lot is in danger of ending up on the floor.

Then, into the oven with the cake, and an anxious wait. It comes out looking just right. What a relief!
'It does smell good,' says Kizzy.
'I wish we could have some now!' adds Dean.

'That's enough: 150 grams,' says Jason as Anthony measures out the dried coconut. They are making coconut ice for the stall.

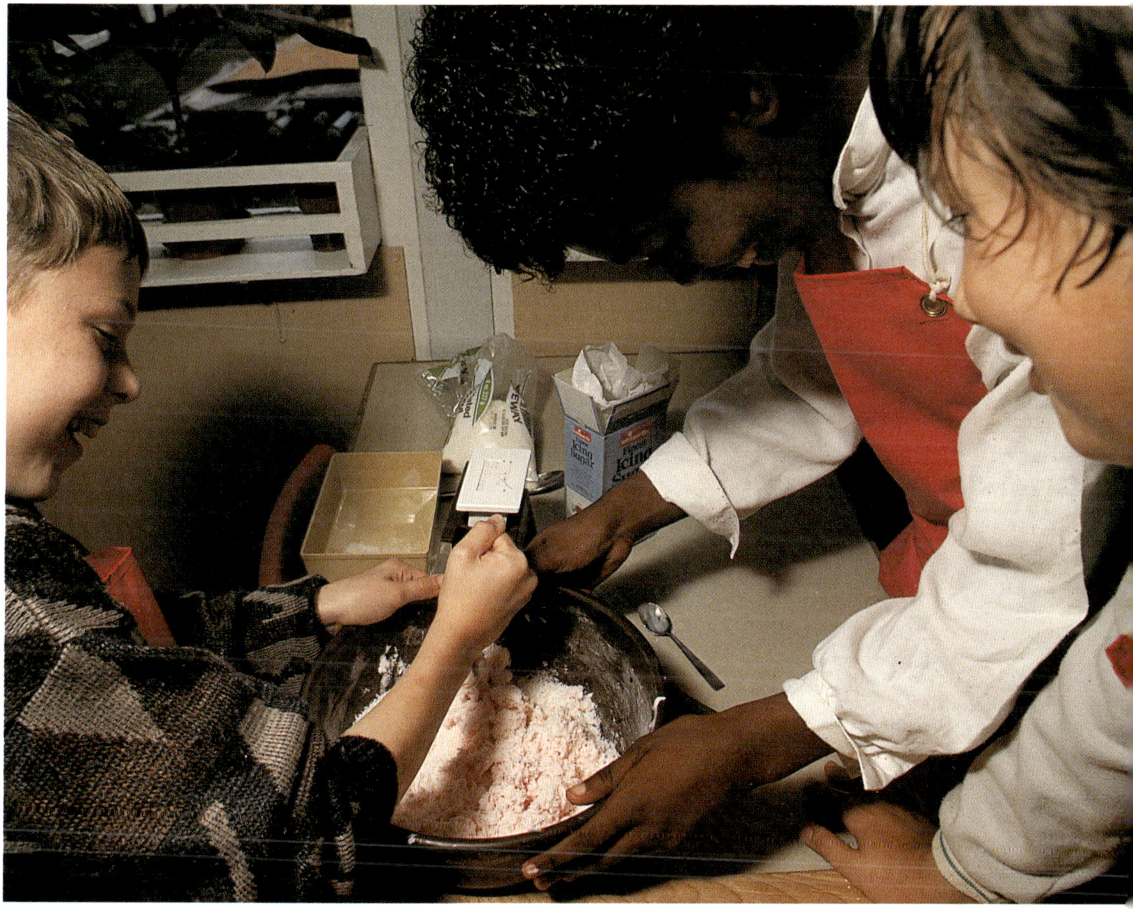

We mix in the milk and icing sugar. Once we've added the pink colour, it does look pretty.

'Don't eat it, Anthony!' yells Muriel.
'*You* ate some!' Anthony answers.
'There won't be any left to sell when you two have finished!' Jason points out.

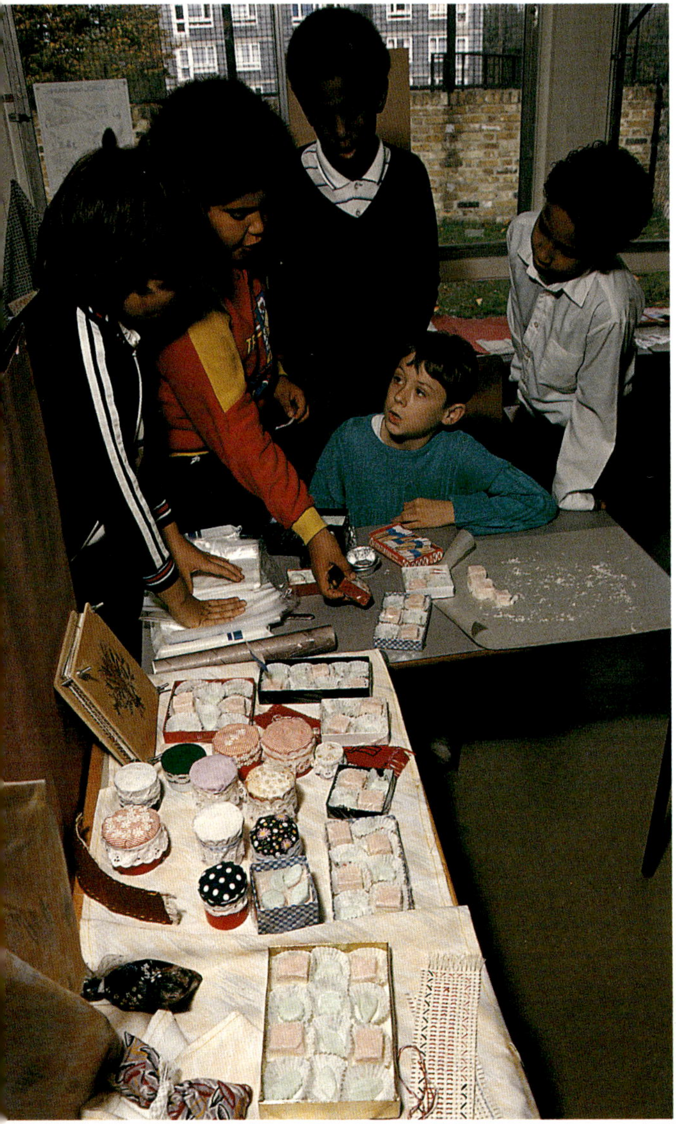

The stall is going to open at half-past two this afternoon. We still have a lot to do. The sweets have to be packed up, and we must decide how much to charge for everything we've made. There is as much discussion about that as about everything else!

After lunch we put on the 'Victorian' clothes we've brought from home. Sally is wearing one of her mum's dresses and Zoë offers to tie the ribbons. Alexia needs help too. 'I can't reach the buttons at the back,' she explains.

Jack and Luke have already dressed up as poor street boys – so they're off to stick the poster on the front door.

We've chosen a sunny spot in the hall to lay out the tables. Already they're looking quite full with the pincushions, bookmarks and needlecases we've made.

‘These look good, don’t they!’ says Jack.

Everyone is beginning to feel a bit nervous. What if no one comes to buy anything?

We needn't have worried. Our first customer arrives! Suddenly there are so many people that we don't know which way to turn first.

Minute by minute the things we have made are bought and carried away. The tables begin to look a little bare.

Our Victorian Stall is nearly over.

'Perhaps . . . ,' says someone, 'perhaps we ought to do something like this again, next term . . .'

Our grateful thanks are due to the children, staff and parents of Paxton Primary School, particularly to Kate Taylor and her Class 7 for sharing their fund-raising efforts with us, and to Brian Marston, headteacher, for allowing us the chance to make this book about their enthusiastic and thoughtful work.

We also owe many thanks to Sarah O'Connor of the NSPCC, whose talk about the work of the Society prompted the children to plan their Victorian Stall.

The photograph on page 3 appears by courtesy of the Mansell Collection.

HAMISH HAMILTON CHILDREN'S BOOKS

Published by the Penguin Group
27 Wrights Lane, London W8 5TZ, England
Viking Penguin Inc, 40 West 23rd Street, New York, New York 10010, U.S.A.
Penguin Books Australia Ltd, Ringwood, Victoria, Australia
Penguin Books Canada Ltd, 2801 John Street, Markham, Ontario, Canada L3R 1B4
Penguin Books (N.Z.) Ltd, 182-190 Wairau Road, Auckland 10, New Zealand

Penguin Books Ltd, Registered Offices: Harmondsworth, Middlesex, England

First published in Great Britain 1990 by
Hamish Hamilton Children's Books

Design by Tony Garrett

1 3 5 7 9 10 8 6 4 2

British Library Cataloguing in Publication Data
CIP data for this book is available from the British Library

ISBN 0-241-12758-0

Printed in Hong Kong by Imago Publishing